GRANDFATHER'S STORY

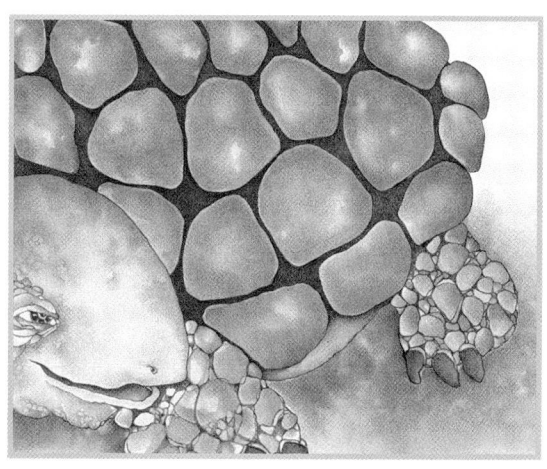

written & illustrated by

BRENDA LENA FAZIO

SASQUATCH BOOKS
SEATTLE

Grandson . . .

When I was a young man,

the birds fished for my catch to feed my family.

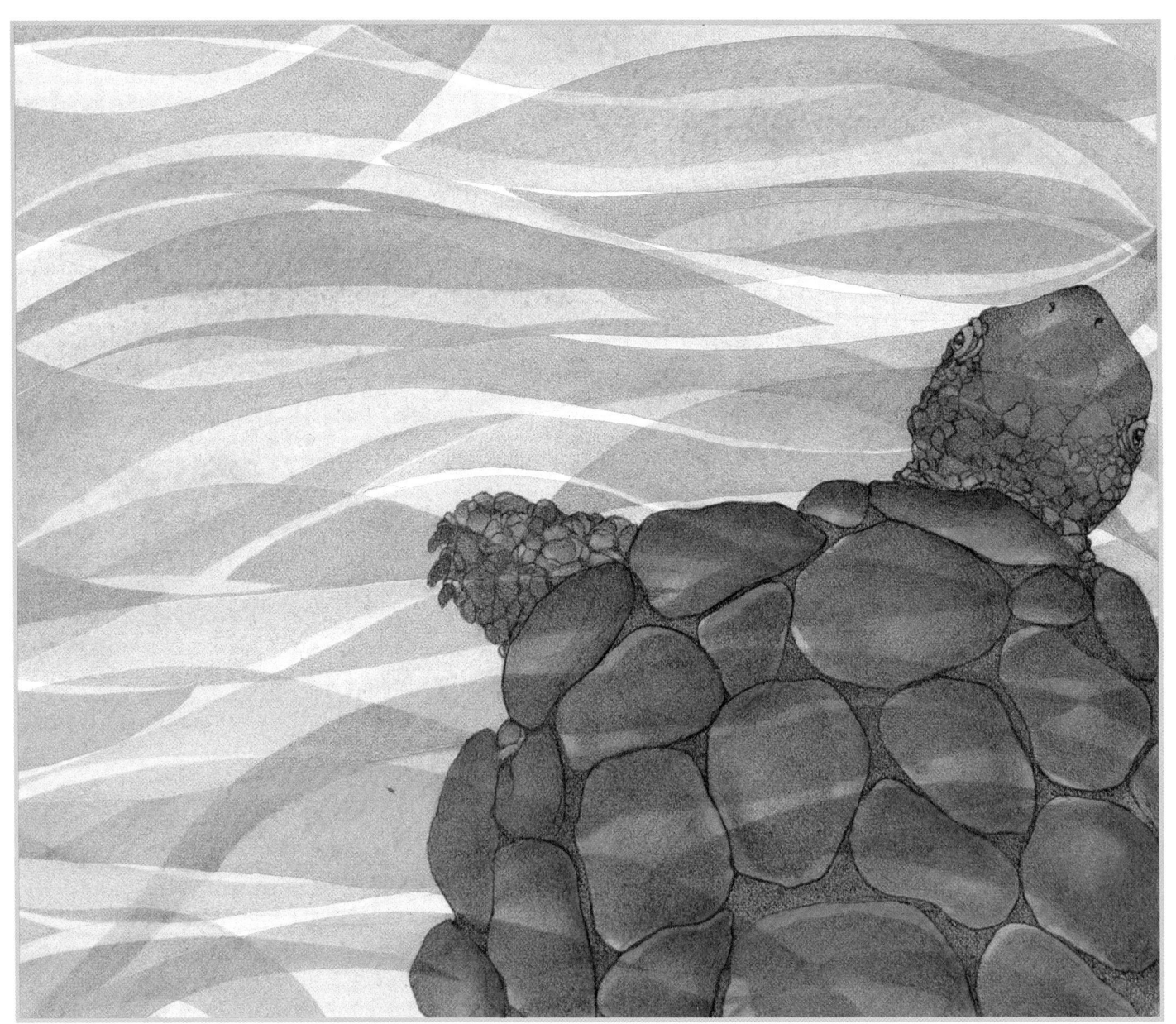

I hunted just enough sea turtles to trade their shells for wood.

With the wood I built my boat.

My boat took me out to sea all day . . .

. . . and in the evening the stars

guided me back to shore.

Now I am an old grandfather

and no longer able to go to sea.

I am of no use to anyone.

But grandson, you will remember all that I have taught you . . .

how to plant a turnip seed and

gently water it until it sprouts.

Grandson, you will remember how I showed you

to care for the birds who once fished for my catch.

Grandson, you will remember always to respect the sea turtles.

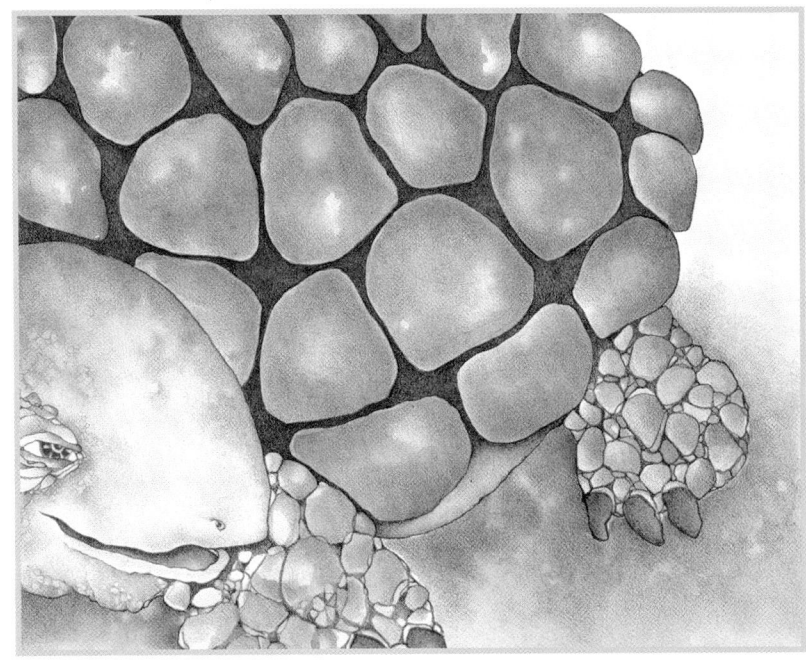

All that you have learned, hold in your memory of me,

for one day I will be gone.

While the grandfather slept that night, he dreamed.

He dreamed he was at sea. His boat rocked and swayed in the rolling waves until he was thrown overboard into the dark swirling water.

As he plunged downward, a giant turtle rose up from the
bottom of the sea and carried the grandfather to shore.

There, the bird who had helped him fish

so long ago was waiting for them.

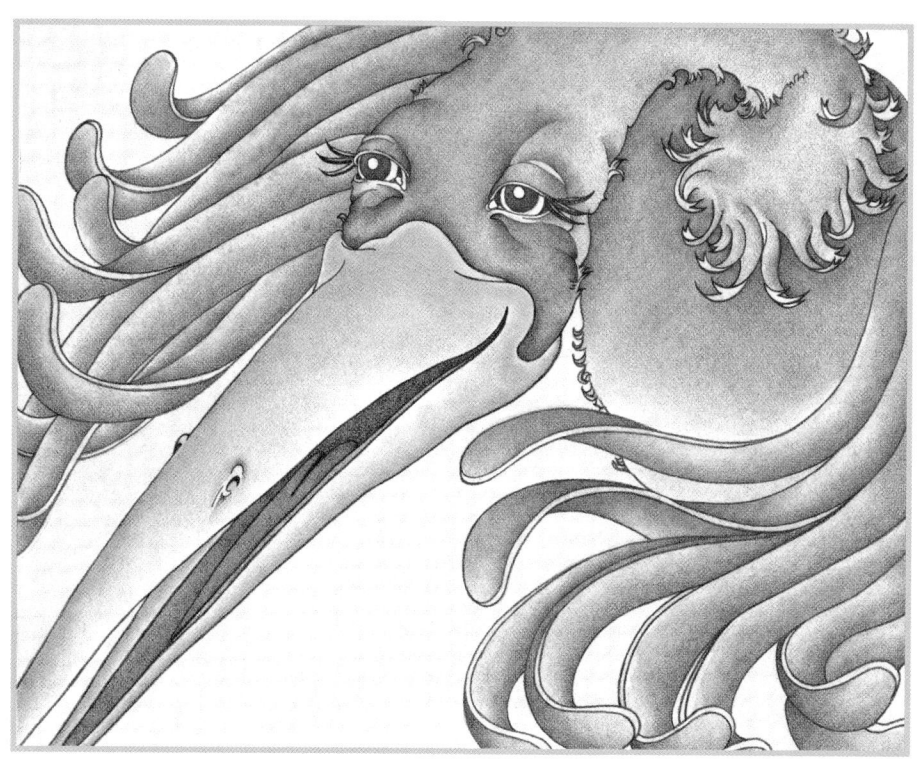

Raising his wings and flapping them back and forth,

the bird dried off the soaking grandfather.

Then to the grandfather's surprise,
the turtle and bird both spoke:

"You, grandfather, have much

yet to teach your grandson.

Now go on your way, go back home."

In the morning when he woke,

the grandfather remembered his dream.

Yes, he said to himself.

There are many things left that I

must share with my grandson.

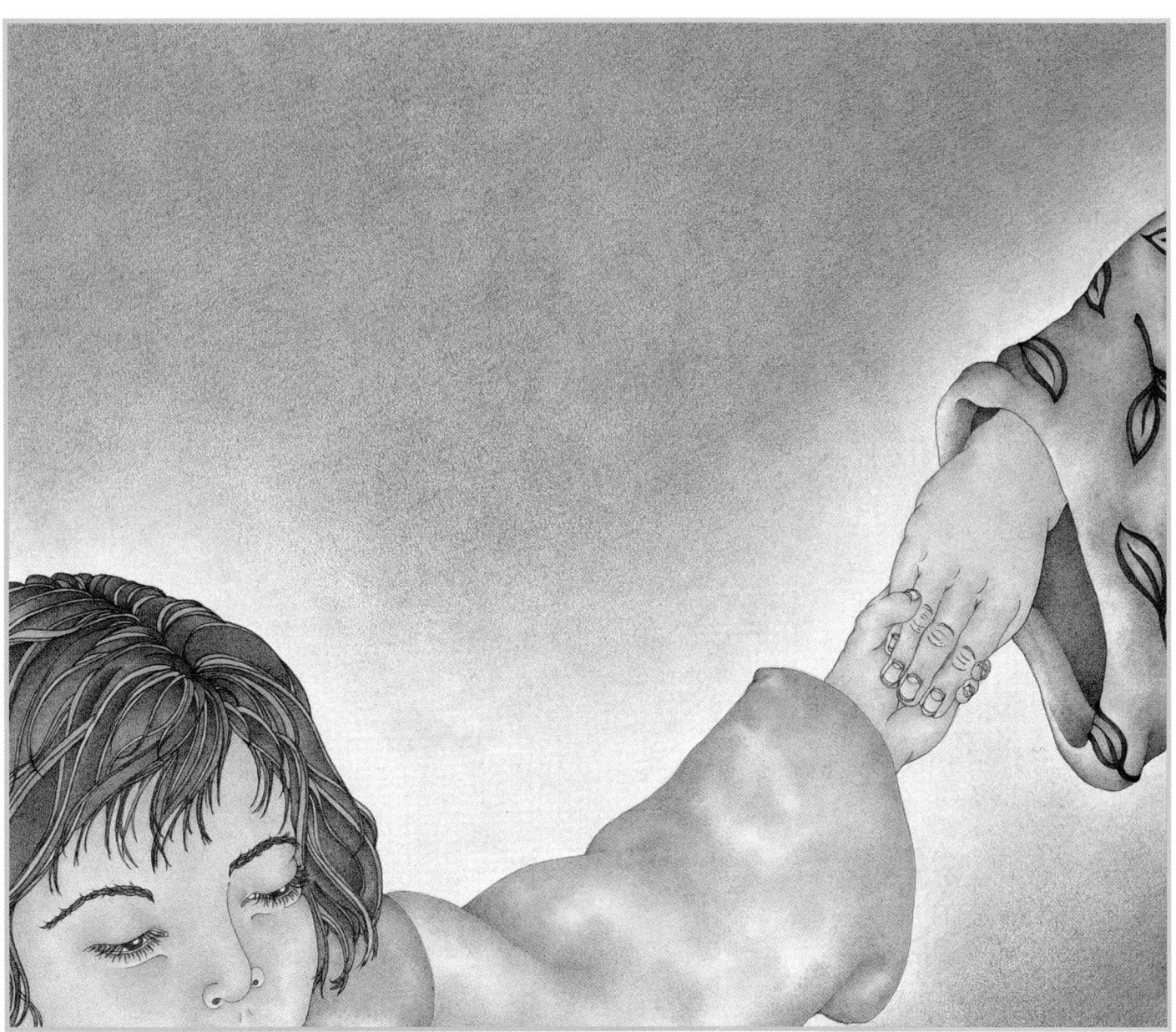

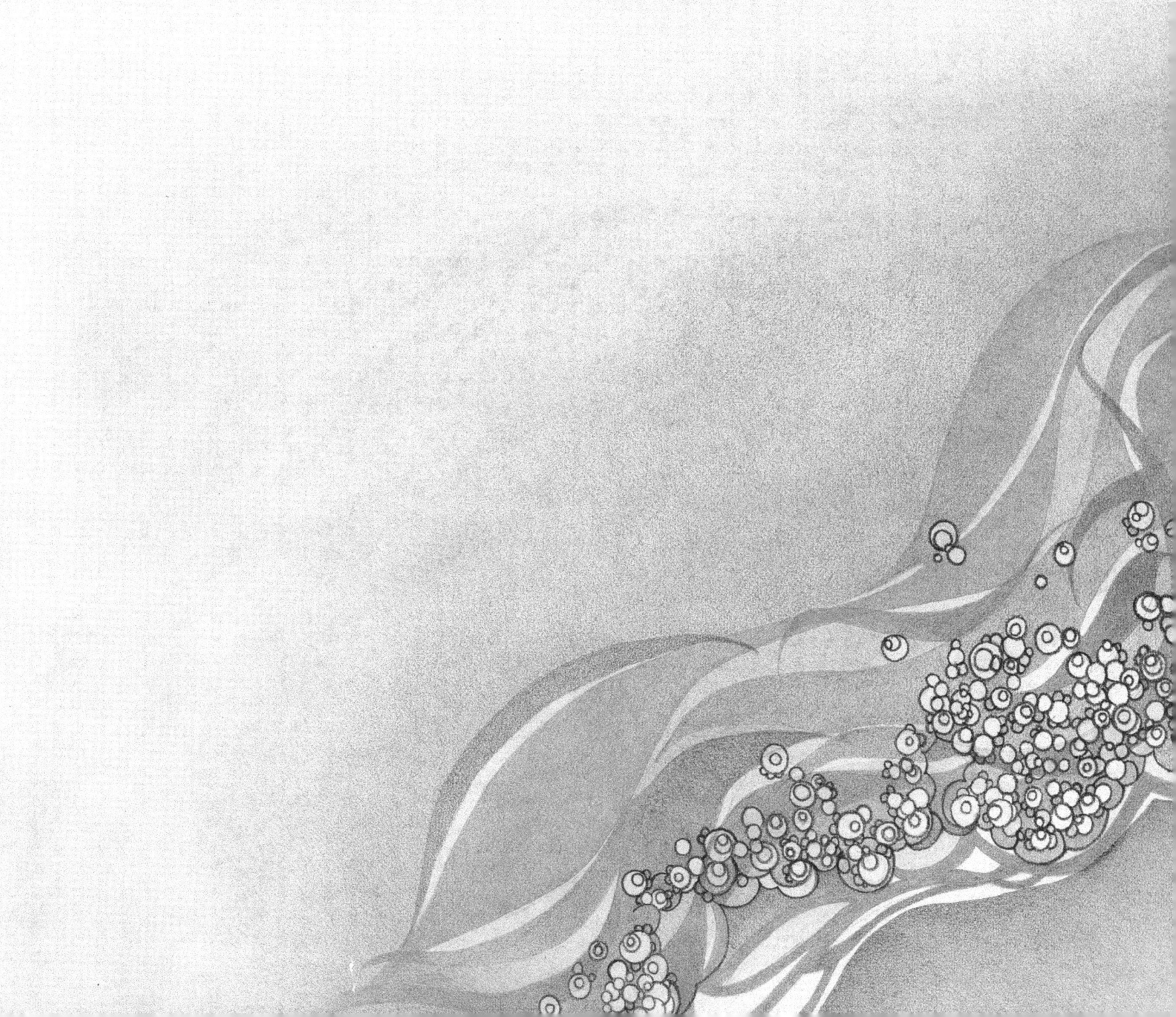

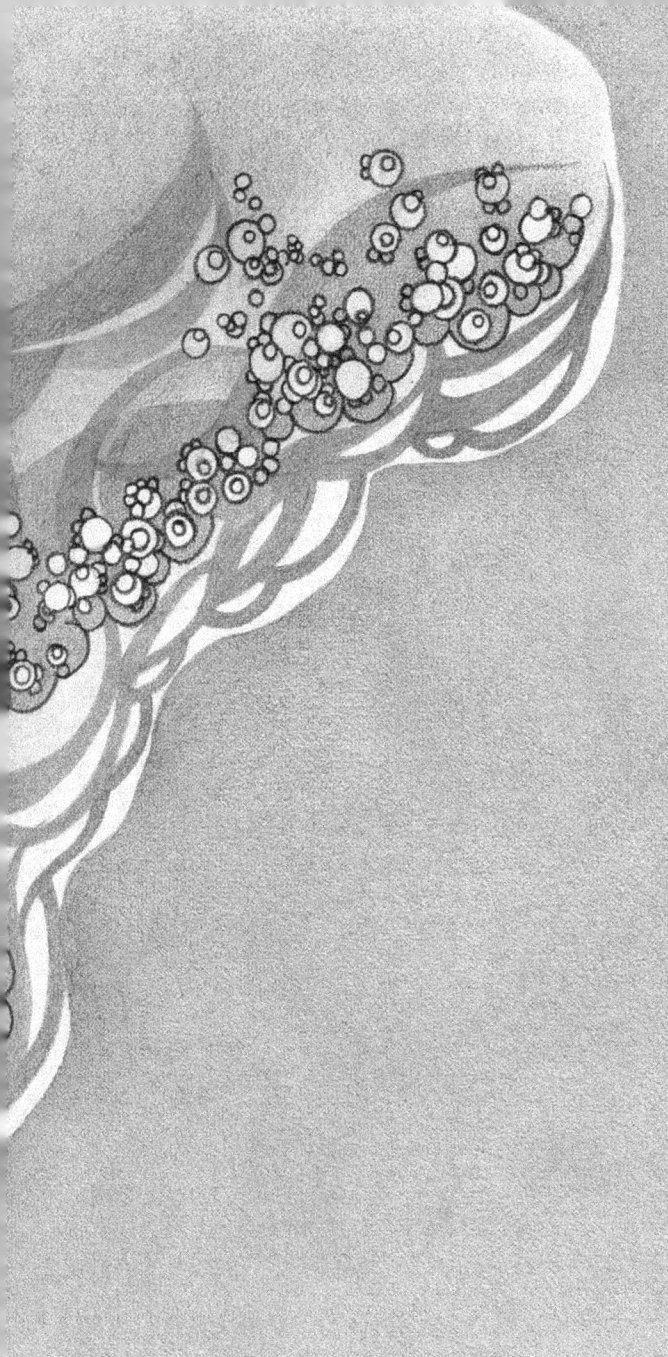

We will start with a walk to the sea.

for mom, dad, gram,
and brothers...
...daniel 2:21

Text and illustrations copyright © 1996 by Brenda Lena Fazio

This book was inspired by an untitled Japanese poem (number 355, "What wretched creatures . . . ")
by Ryojin-hisho found in *The Dance of the Dust on Rafters* (Broken Moon Press, 1990).

Published by Sasquatch Books
Distributed in Canada by Raincoast Books Ltd.

Printed in Hong Kong
Designed by Karen Schober
Text set in Eva Antiqua

Library of Congress Cataloging-in-Publication Data

Fazio, Brenda Lena, 1968-
    Grandfather's story / written & illustrated by Brenda Lena Fazio.
              p.   cm.
Summary: A dream reminds a grandfather how much he has yet to share with his grandson.
ISBN 1-57061-028-2 (cloth)
[1. Grandfathers—Fiction. 2. Japan—Fiction.] I. Title.
PZ7.F2925Gr   1996
[E]—dc20   95-52203

Sasquatch Books
1008 Western Avenue • Seattle, Washington 98104
(206)467-4300 • books@sasquatchbooks.com • http://www.sasquatch.com

Sasquatch Books publishes high-quality adult nonfiction and children's books related to the Northwest (San Francisco to Alaska).
For information about our books, contact us at the above address, or view our site on the World Wide Web.